What shall I paint?

Ray Gibson

Designed by Amanda Barlow

Illustrated by Michaela Kennard

Edited By Felicity Everett

Series Editor: Jenny Tyler

Contents

Paint a parrot

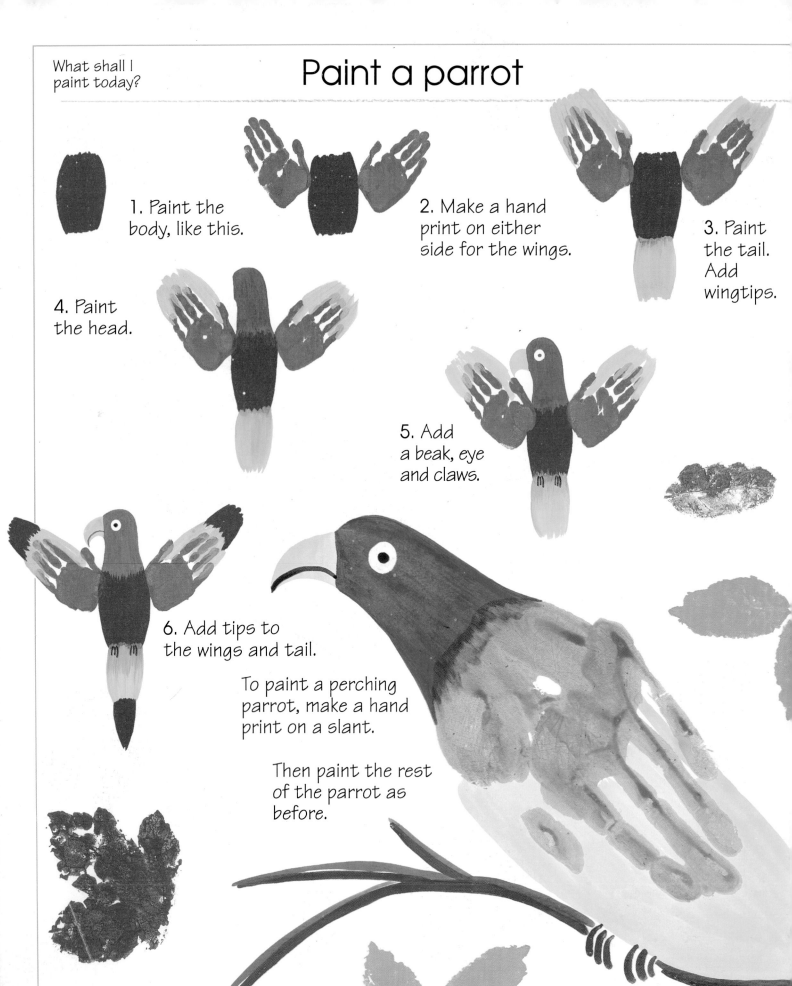

1. Paint the
body, like this.

2. Make a hand
print on either
side for the wings.

3. Paint
the tail.
Add
wingtips.

4. Paint
the head.

5. Add
a beak, eye
and claws.

6. Add tips to
the wings and tail.

To paint a perching
parrot, make a hand
print on a slant.

Then paint the rest
of the parrot as
before.

  Now how about... a row of perching parrots on a long branch?

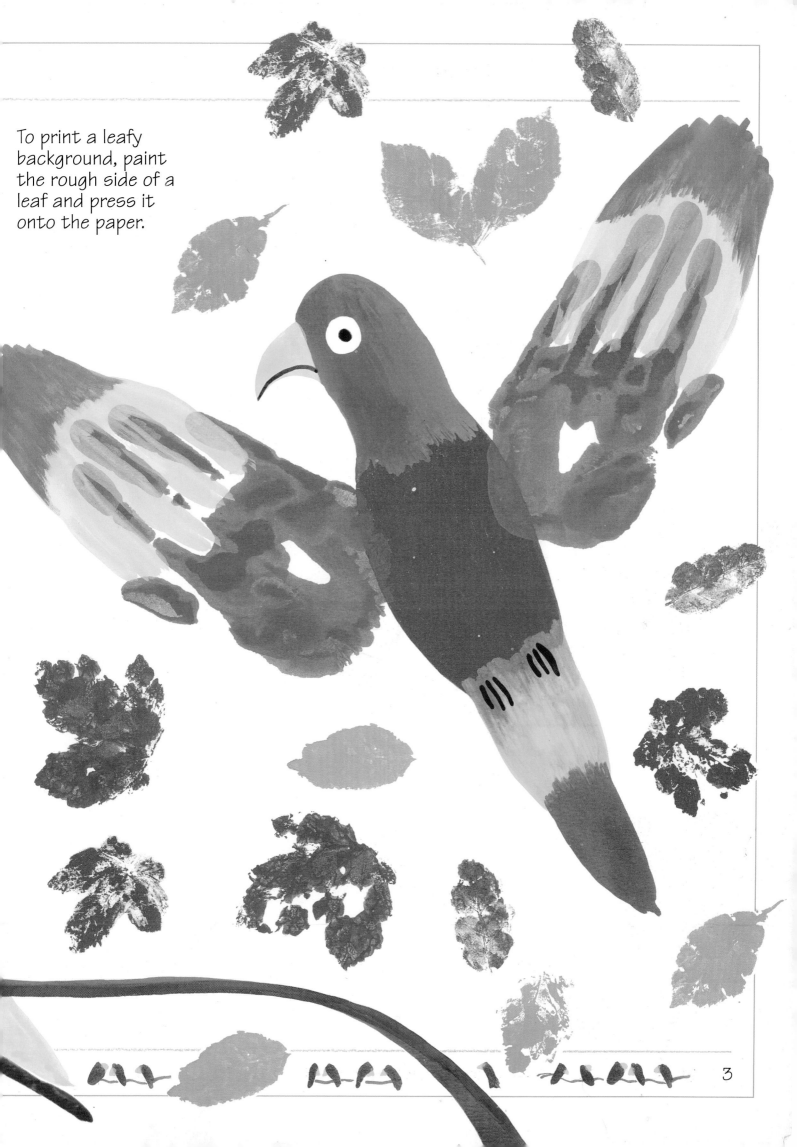

To print a leafy
background, paint
the rough side of a
leaf and press it
onto the paper.

3

Paint a cat on a rug

1. Draw a cat's head in crayon near one side of your sheet of paper.

2. Now draw its body. Add a face, tail and whiskers. Go over the lines again.

3. With a new crayon, draw a big oblong around the cat. Add stripes and patterns.

4. Now paint over the cat, using runny black paint. The cat will show through.

5. Paint the rug area in different shades. The patterns will show through.

6. Crayon a fringe at both ends of your rug to finish off the picture.

You could use only one shade of paint for the rug.

A cat in the grass

Draw a cat with a yellow crayon. Crayon flowers around it. Paint over the cat with orange paint and over the flowers with green paint.

Now how about... a window with patterned curtains?   5

Paint a monster

1. Fold your paper in half. Press down firmly and then open it.

2. With a damp cloth, wipe on some blue paint for the sky.

3. Paint a tree shape down one side. Fold your paper again and press down firmly.

4. When you open it, there will be trees down both edges of the paper. Allow to dry.

5. Paint some blobs near the middle of the paper like this. Use monster-ish shades.

6. Fold and press the paper again. Open it out. When the paint is dry, add eyes and teeth.

Now how about... an alien?

Paint a scary picture

Haunted woods

1. Fold your paper in half. Press down firmly, then open it out again.

2. With a damp cloth, wipe on some red and yellow paint.

3. Paint trees on one side with runny black paint. Fold and press.

4. When dry, paint scary eyes among your spooky trees.

A dragon

1. Fold your paper in half, press down firmly and open it out again.

2. Paint some blobs near the middle. Fold and press, then open the paper.

3. Paint the head, legs and tail when dry.

Eyes

Teeth

Now how about... a shaggy dog?

Paint penguins on the ice

Ice

Sea

Icy sea

1. With a damp cloth, wipe white paint over one end of the paper.

2. In the same way, wipe blue paint over the rest of it.

3. Paint some clingwrap white. Press the painted side over the blue.

4. Lift it off gently and repeat until all the blue is patterned with white.

Penguins

Beak

Eye

Feet

1. Paint a body.

2. Add wings.

3. Let the paint dry.

4. Add a tummy.

Fish

1.

2.

3.

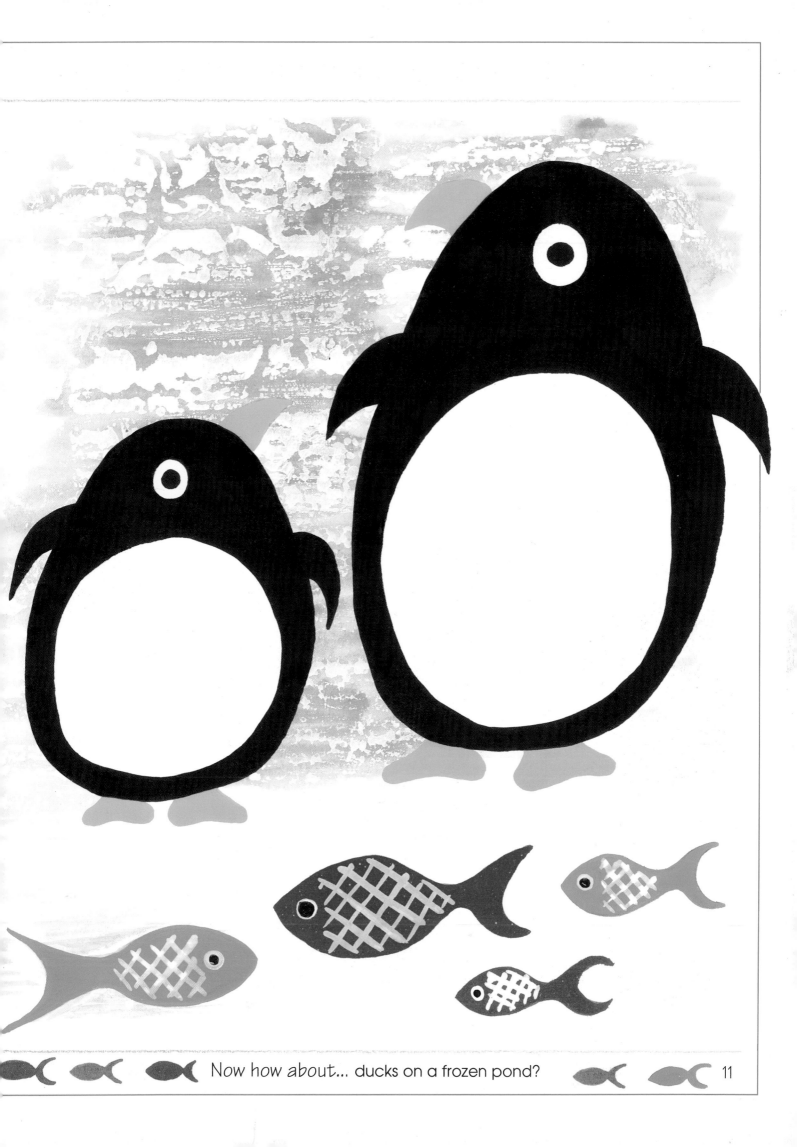

Now how about... ducks on a frozen pond?

Paint flowers

Poppies

1. Make some swirly petal shapes with a pale candle.

2. Paint over them like this.

Daisies

1. Draw loopy petal shapes with the candle.

2. Paint over them like this.

Tulips

1. Draw upright petal shapes with the candle.

2. Paint over them like this.

Buds

1. Draw small squiggles with the candle.

2. Paint over them like this.

Now how about... a big hat with flowers on it?

Paint a truck

1. Take an oblong sponge and dip the end in paint. Press it onto your paper.

2. Carefully print two more oblongs on either side of the first one.

3. For the engine, print a fourth oblong on its side in front of the first three.

Paint a busy road

Now try painting lots of trucks, vans and buses.

Use the big side of your sponge to print this van.

For the bus, use the long, narrow side of the sponge.

This small truck has three wheels.

You could add some road signs to your picture.

4. For the driver's cab, dip the end of a matchbox in paint and print two lines.

5. Use a round, cut potato to print wheels. Print a headlight using the end of a cork.

6. To make the road, dip crumpled paper in grey paint and press it along the paper under your truck.

It's fun to make up signs of your own.

Print windows with the end of a matchbox.

Use a matchbox to print the three oblongs on the front.

Paint a bonfire

1. Take a piece of black paper and some runny yellow paint. Paint a bonfire shape.

2. Using runny red paint, add some wiggly stripes to your bonfire shape.

3. Using your fingers, mix the paint together to make flames.

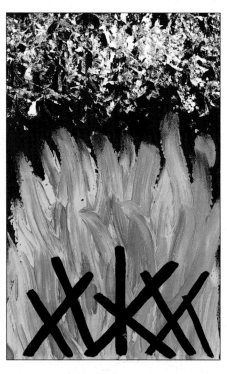

6. Splash on some big sparks with your paintbrush. It's best to do this outside.

4. Crumple up some paper and dip it in white paint. Dab it on for the smoke.

5. Paint black sticks and logs. Don't worry if the paints mix.

Now how about... a firework display?

Paint a cactus in the desert

1. Paint a wiggly line for sand at the bottom of very large paper.

2. With a damp cloth, wipe on some paint for the sky.

3. In the same way wipe on some red streaks for clouds.

4. Paint the bottom of a clean rubber shoe or boot. Press it onto your paper.

5. Make more overlapping shoe prints. Repaint the shoe each time.

6. Add pink flowers and a bright sun with a paintbrush.

7. Dip your fingers in orange paint and print some stones.

Cactus

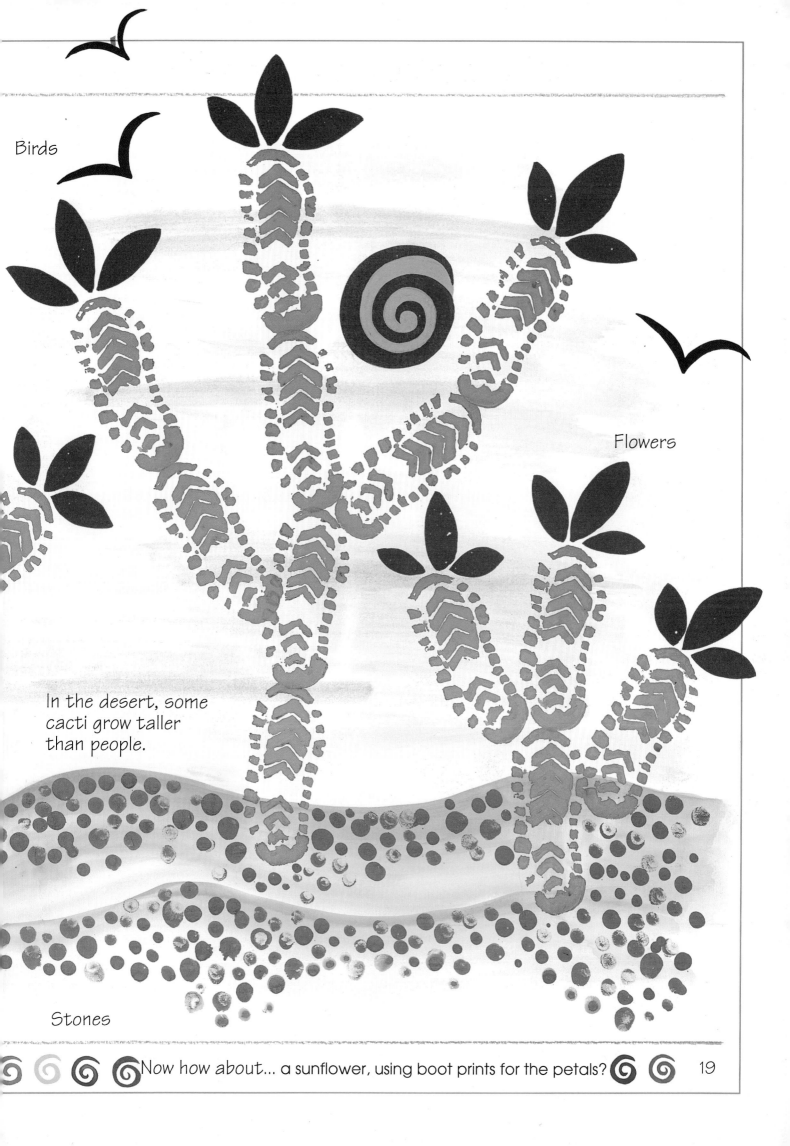

Birds

Flowers

In the desert, some cacti grow taller than people.

Stones

Paint a sky picture

1. Cut cloud shapes out of scrap paper. Lay them on a large sheet of thick paper.

2. With a damp sponge, gently dab blue paint around the edges of all your clouds.

3. When the whole sheet of paper is covered with blue, peel the clouds off gently.

4. Paint some hot air balloons in the sky. Add some planes doing exciting stunts.

5. When the planes and balloons have dried, decorate them with bright patterns.

6. Add smoke trails to the planes using a piece of damp sponge dipped in paint.

Now how about... kites in the sky?

Paint sheep in a field

3. Wind some yarn or wool around an old birthday card. You don't need to wind it very neatly. When the card is covered, tape down the end and cut off the leftover yarn.

1. Draw sheep's bodies and lambs' bodies on pieces of scrap paper. Cut them out.

2. Dip them in water. Shake off the drops, then arrange them on your painting paper.

4. Paint the yarn green on one side. Press it all over your paper. Add more paint as you go.

5. Gently peel off the paper sheep. Paint on faces and legs with a fine paintbrush.

6. Add some flowers. Print them with a fingertip.

Paint a face

1. Ask a
grown-up to
cut a big
potato in
half.

2. Dip the
cut half of
the potato in
some paint.
Print a face
with it.

3. Mix some
runny paint.
Pour some
along the top
of your
printed face.

4. For hair, blow through
a straw onto the paint.

5. Print the eyes with a
finger dipped in paint.

Add long hair and a
crown for a princess.

6. Paint the nose
and the mouth.

Add ears that
stick out and a
round mouth for a baby.

Now how about... some animals, using potato prints for the bodies?

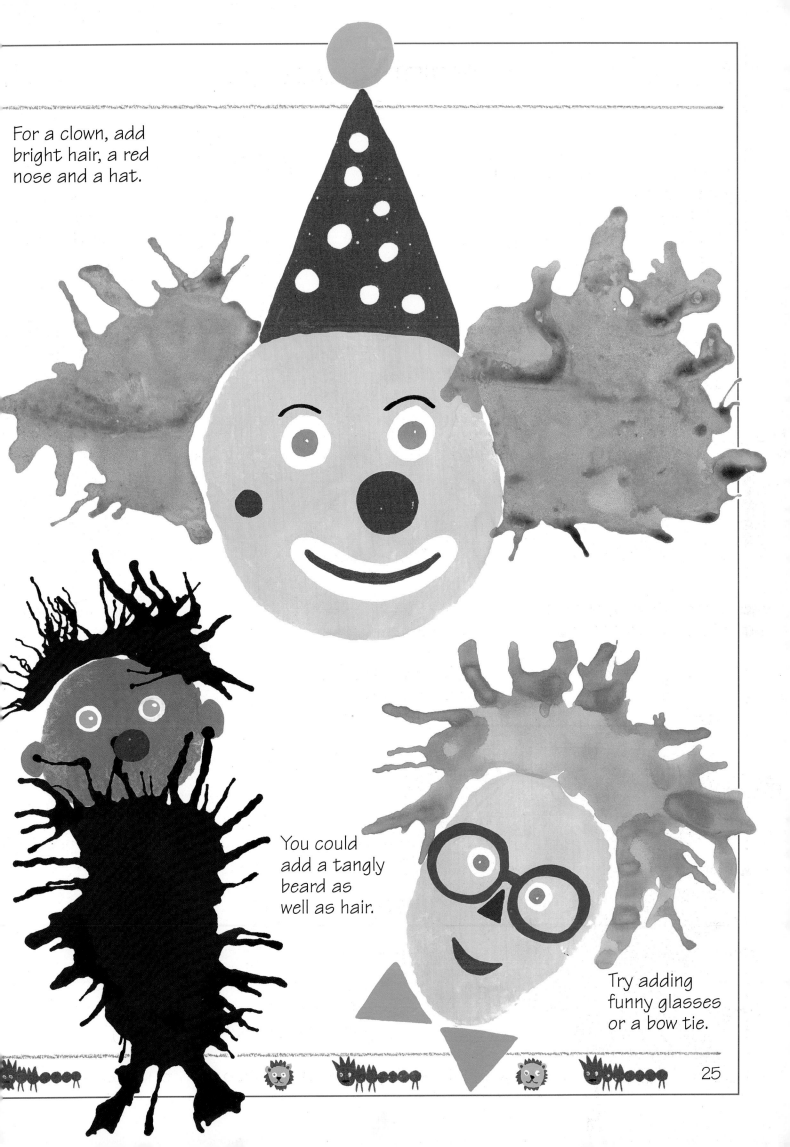

For a clown, add bright hair, a red nose and a hat.

You could add a tangly beard as well as hair.

Try adding funny glasses or a bow tie.

Paint a scarecrow

1. Dip a damp cloth in brown paint. Wipe it over about half your paper.

2. Still using a damp cloth wipe blue paint over the rest of your paper.

3. With a clean damp cloth blot some of the blue paint off again.

4. Thicken yellow paint with some flour. Finger-paint rows of corn.

5. With thick paint, finger-paint a turnip-shaped head. Add a stick body.

6. Now finger-paint some clothes. Add eyes and a mouth and a carrot nose.

7. Dip the edge of some cardboard in yellow paint. Print some straw hair.

Paint pigs in some straw

Paint some pigs. You could use your fingers or a paint brush.

Print the straw with the edge of some cardboard.

Now how about... some birds in a nest?

Paint fish in a waterfall

1. With a damp cloth,
wipe blue stripes down
your paper.

2. Add some green
stripes to your paper
in the same way.

3. Make white
handprints along the
bottom of your paper.

4. Splash some white
paint on with a brush
to look like spray.

5. On another piece of
paper paint lots of
bright fish.

6. Let the paint
dry. Add patterns
on top.

7. Cut the fish
out. Glue them
onto the waterfall
picture.

Now how about... an underwater picture with handprints for seaweed?

Paint a pattern

1. Mix flour with two different shades of paint to make it really thick.

2. Cut an old postcard in half. Cut V shapes all along one of the shorter edges.

3. Take a big sheet of thick paper. Paint some thick stripes on it using two shades.

4. Scrape lots of different patterns into the painted stripes using the straight end of the card.

5. Then scrape patterns into the stripes using the zig zag end of the card. Make some straight and some wavy.

Butterfly

1. Paint thickly over a big sheet of paper.

3. Use a pencil to draw half a butterfly shape against the fold. Trace over the shape with your finger, pressing hard.

2. Fold in half, painted side in.

4. Open it out.

To change a pattern, paint over it and start again.

Paint more patterns

1. Fold a sheet of kitchen towel in half and in half again.

2. Fold it in half twice more, pressing hard.

3. Dip the corners into runny paint.

4. Put the folded kitchen towel between some sheets of newspaper. Roll over hard, with a rolling pin.

5. Take out the kitchen towel and open it very gently.

Other shapes

Fold a piece of towel into a triangle and dip the sides or the corners.

Fold a piece of towel into a rectangle and dip each side of it in paint.

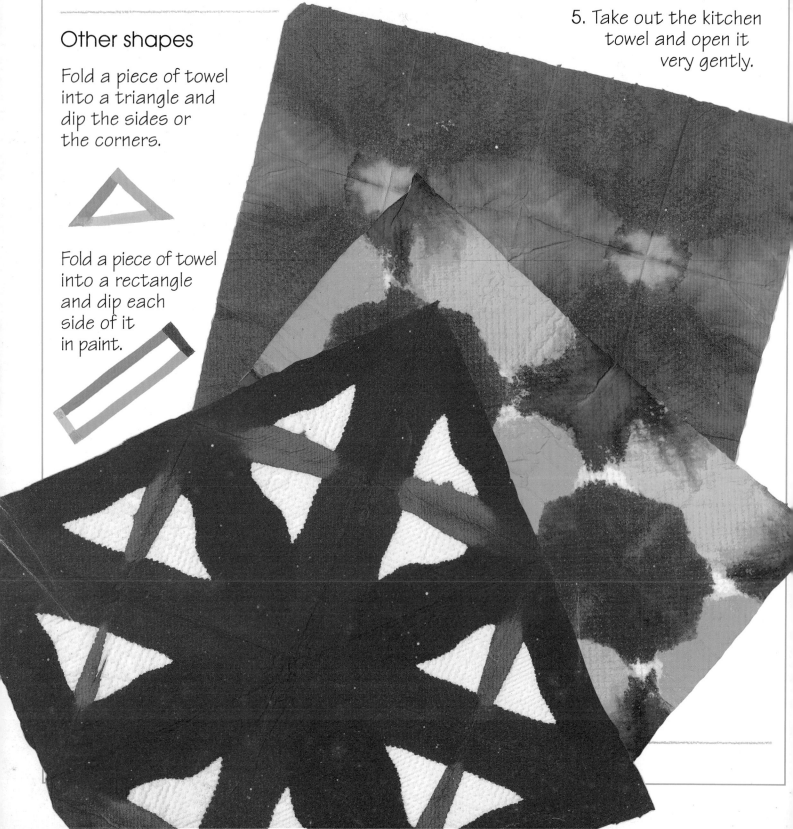